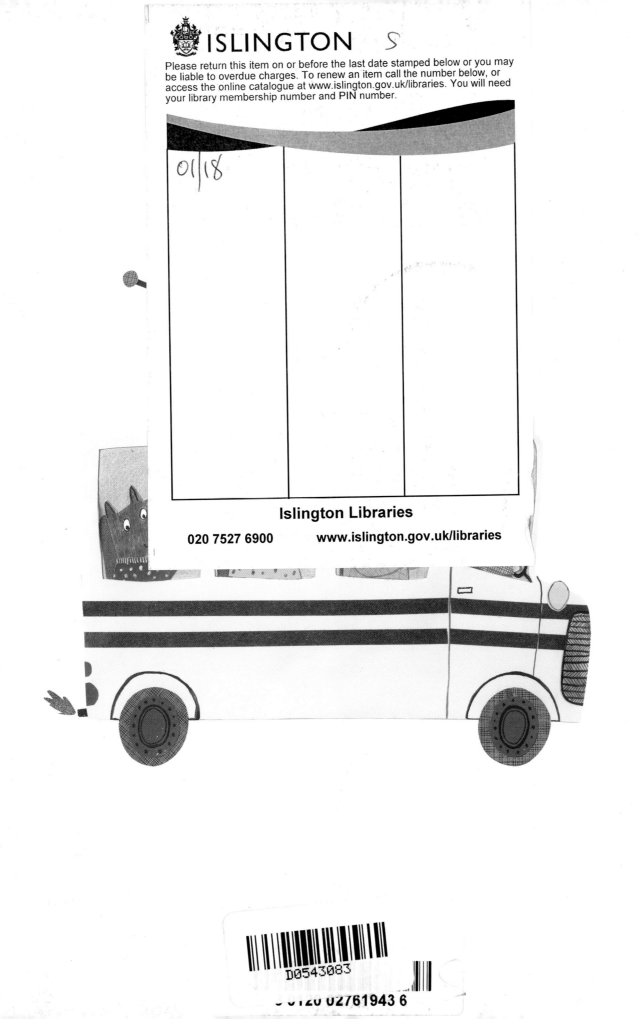

ISLINGTON S

Please return this item on or before the last date stamped below or you may be liable to overdue charges. To renew an item call the number below, or access the online catalogue at www.islington.gov.uk/libraries. You will need your library membership number and PIN number.

01/18

Islington Libraries

020 7527 6900   www.islington.gov.uk/libraries

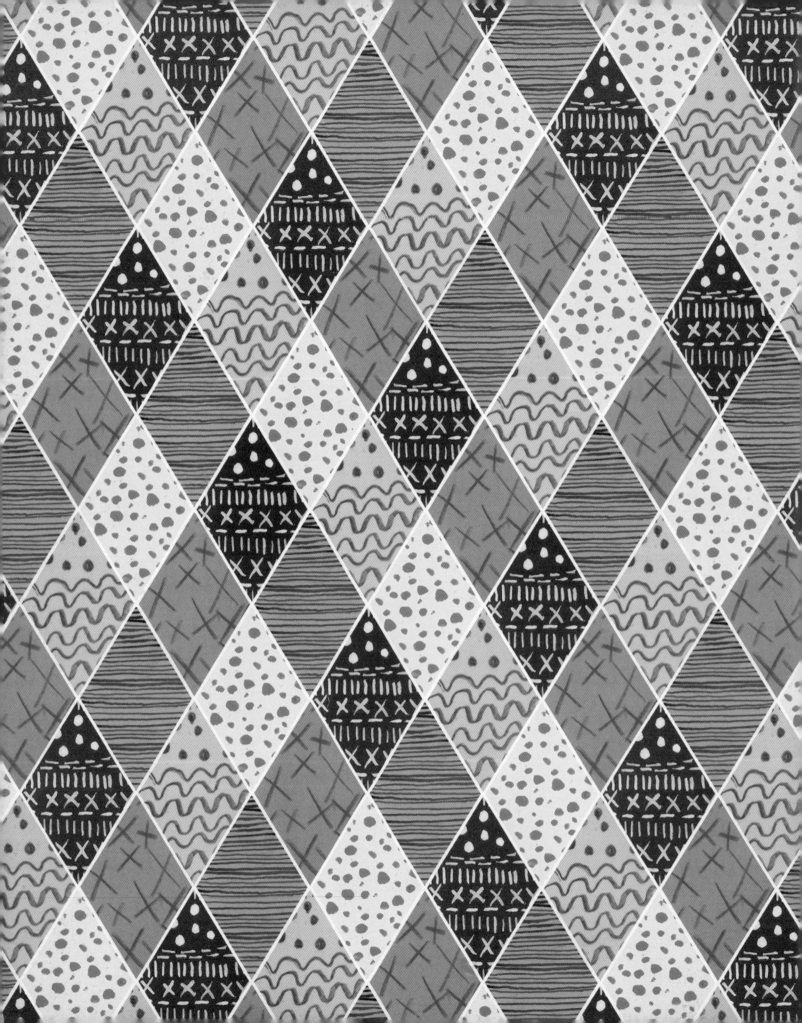

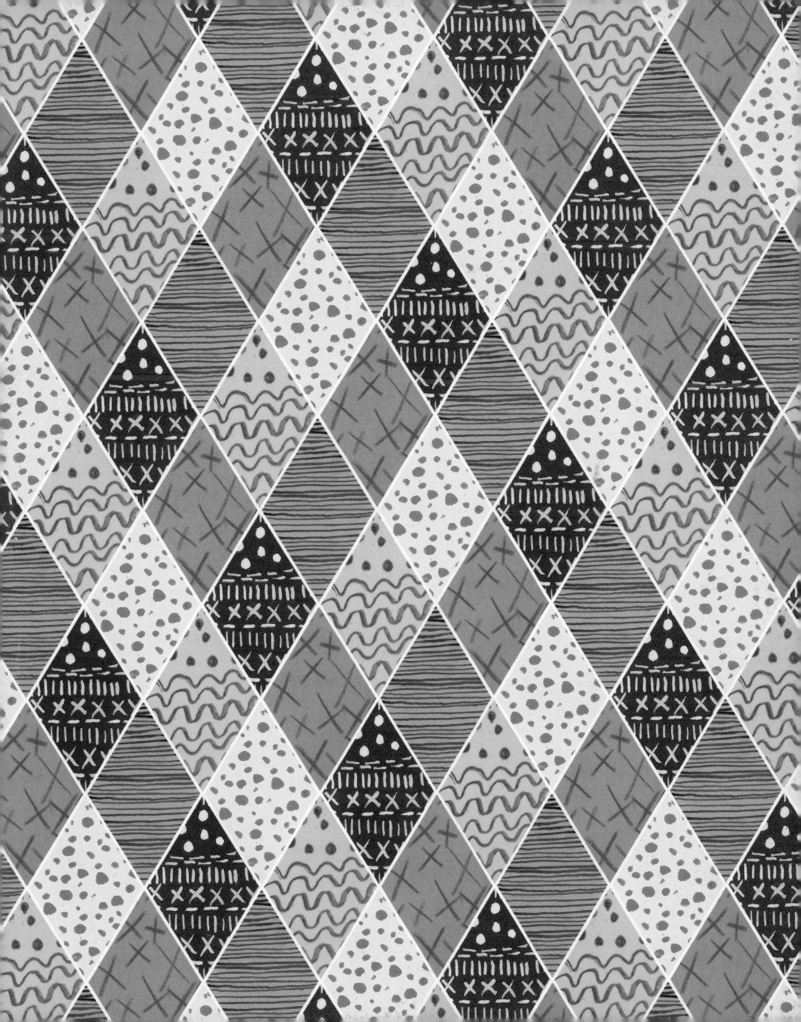

Willow
Tree

A CIP catalogue record for this book is
available from the British Library

This edition published by Willow Tree Books, 2018
Willow Tree Books, Tide Mill Way, Woodbridge, Suffolk, IP12 1AP

0 2 4 6 8 9 7 5 3 1

Text © 2014 Amy Husband
Illustration © 2014 Amy Husband

Willow Tree Books and associated logos are trademarks and/or
registered trademarks of Tide Mill Media Ltd

Written and illustrated by Amy Husband

ISBN: 978-1-78700-463-4
Manufactured in China

www.willowtreebooks.net

'For Dad, who inspired this story'

THE NOISY FOXES

Amy Husband

In a **very noisy** house in a **very noisy** city lived three **noisy** foxes.

They spent
ALL DAY
being
very noisy ...

mixing ...
fixing ...

hopping and
bopping ...

banging
and
clanging.

'Wouldn't it be nice to be quiet sometimes?' asked Fox Number One.

'Perhaps we should move to the countryside,' suggested Fox Number Two.

'What a good idea!' replied Fox Number Three.

So they packed up all of their **very noisy** things,
and caught the **very noisy** bus, to find a place
to live in the very quiet countryside.

Twit-twoo!

In a very quiet **wood**, **in the** very quiet **countryside**, they met an owl.

'Twit-twoo. Who are you?' hooted the owl.

'We are from the **very noisy** city, looking for a quiet place to live,' replied Fox Number One. 'Where do you live, Owl?'

'I live up here at the top of this very tall, quiet tree,' the owl said.

'Oh yes, it is very quiet, but it is too high for us,' said Fox Number One. 'We're scared!'

Next, in a very quiet meadow, in the very quiet countryside, the noisy foxes met a mole, who popped up out of the ground.

'Hello, Mole. We are from the noisy city looking for a quiet place to live. Can you help us?' asked Fox Number Two.

'Oh yes, I live in a very quiet place,' replied the mole. 'Follow me and I'll show you.'

'I live here in this very quiet hole underground,' said the mole.

'Oh yes, it is very quiet, but it is too dark for us,' said Fox Number Two. 'We can't see!'

... AND I'M STUCK!

In a very quiet **clearing, in the** very quiet countryside, the **noisy** foxes met a frog.

'Ribbit, ribbit. What do you three **noisy** foxes want?' the frog asked.

'We are looking for a quiet place to live,' said Fox Number Three. 'Where do you live, Frog?'

'Come with me and I'll show you,' replied the frog.

'I live here in this very quiet pond,' said the frog.

'Oh yes, it is very quiet indeed, but it is too wet for us,' said Fox Number Three. 'And we can't swim!'

So the three noisy foxes kept searching for a very, very long time and they ended up in the very quietest part of the countryside, a long, long way from the very noisy city. As they ventured along the very quiet path, they met a badger.

'Hello, Badger. We are looking for a quiet place to live,' said the noisy foxes. 'Can you help us? We have looked everywhere.'

'Yes, of course. Follow me,' replied the badger.

'This is where I live,' said the badger.
'It is the quietest place in all of the countryside.'

'Oh yes, it really is very quiet, and very lovely.
It might just be the perfect place,' said the
noisy foxes. 'But ...

... it is just TOO quiet!'

The **noisy** foxes were
really fed up with being quiet!
So they started to make some noise.
As they banged and clanged and chittered
and chattered, a quiet little mouse scurried up to them.

'What is all this noise about?' asked the quiet little mouse.

'We need a place to live, but it can't be too high, it can't
be too dark, it can't be too wet, and it definitely can't
be too quiet,' replied the **noisy** foxes.

'I know the perfect place,'
Squeaked the mouse. 'Follow me.'

'Well done, little mouse. This really is the perfect place!'